*Dedicated to children
in the hope that they will grow
in wisdom and knowledge.
In so doing, may they
perceive the truth
that family and friends
are the center of love and
true success in life.*

The Brave Donkey, The Cowardly Lion and The Clever Fox©
Published by Parrot Productions Publishing Company LTD.

Registration Numbers TXU 649-106 - 9/22/94 PA 806-720 - 2/9/96
United States Copyright Office. The Library Of Congress.
ISBN 1-890571-30-X

To the Parents

Welcome to Tootee's Magical Paradise! Who is Tootee? Well, she's the most beautiful bird a child can imagine - and what could be more beautiful than that which comes from the mind of a child?

Tootee wants to help children grow up with beautiful, positive principles, so she flies from Land to Land collecting stories from all over the world to tell the children... stories that come from different cultures. Tootee always tells stories that bring to children positive principles for successful living, designed to encourage them to get along with one another, and to appreciate, respect and accept the differences that make each of us unique.

These principles are brought to life through friendly, animal-world characters and in a way that children enjoy, understand and imitate. In The Brave Donkey, The Cowardly Lion and The Clever Fox, the brave young donkey, Daniel, believes he is ready to face the world on his own, but when he leaves home, even though he is very intelligent, he encounters difficulties that are too great for him.

Through the help of Hartley, the cowardly lion, and Wiley, the clever fox, he learns the importance of family and the value of forgiveness. Daniel goes home a winner, as do all the characters in all of Tootee's stories.

The stories in the Tootee books are the same as those told in the Tootee's Paradise children's television programs that are enhanced with music and dance. The stories are also available on audio and video cassette so that children of all ages may enjoy and learn from them.

Tootee's Magical Stories
The Brave Donkey, The Cowardly Lion, and The Clever Fox

Adapted From A Persian Folktale
by
Kambiz Azordegan

Illustrated by
Johnny Sajem

The Brave Donkey, The Cowardly Lion, and The Clever Fox

Teaches:

the value of forgiveness, confidence and courage.

My name is

_____

This is my book.
Will you please read it to me?

Once upon a time, there was a brave young donkey named Daniel, who lived with his family in a comfortable stable.

In that stable, there was always enough hay to eat, and lots of clean fresh water to drink.

Even though Daniel loved his home and family very much, he longed to leave the stable and explore the world on his own.

Daniel believed that if he could be on his own, he would not have to follow any rules, and no one would tell him what to do all the time.

One night when his family was asleep, Daniel ran away to the dense jungle, where he dreamed of living free like the jungle beasts.

For a while, he had fun. Because there was no one to look after him, he played all day and did *just as he pleased.*

One day, Daniel was frightened by a ferocious noise.

He knew the noise was the roar of a lion - *the King of the Beasts!*

"I must act brave,
or that lion will have
me for dinner!"
Daniel thought quickly.

"I will make a loud noise of
my own so the lion will think
I'm bigger than him."

Daniel bellowed out a very loud
and fierce, "HEE-HAW!"

The lion, whose name was Hartley, was so startled by the noise, he ran out from the bushes, right into Daniel!

"What kind of animal makes such a terrible noise?" asked Hartley. "Who are you?"

Daniel saw that the lion was as scared as he was. He replied, in a deep and powerful voice, **"Who are *you*, and what are *you* doing here?"**

"Oh, my name is Hartley, and I am here to *serve* you!" whimpered Hartley.

"Well," boomed Daniel, "my name is **Lion Hunter**, and you shall be my servant! Here's my rule: make **three mistakes**, and you shall be banished from the jungle *forever*!"

"Yes, yes! I understand and will obey your rule!" cried Hartley. Daniel knew he'd better use the rule to get rid of Hartley before the lion discovered that he was just a donkey.

After that Daniel gave the orders and Hartley obeyed.

The first day, Hartley
saw some flies buzzing abou
Daniel's head as he slept.
"I'd better shoo these flies away so they
won't bother the Lion Hunter, "said Hartley

He shooed
them away.

As he did, Daniel woke up. "What have you done?" he demanded. "I ordered those flies to buzz around my head and sing me to sleep. *That's your first mistake!*"

On the second day, as Daniel and Hartley walked through the jungle, Daniel accidentally stepped in some quicksand. "I'll save you Lion Hunter!" Hartley cried. "I'm very strong!" He quickly pulled Daniel from the quicksand.

"You have insulted me!" Daniel thundered. "I am stronger than you! I didn't need your help! *That's your second mistake!*"

The third day, Daniel and Hartley were walking by a river.

Daniel became thirsty, but as he leaned down for a drink, he fell in!

"Oh, no!" Hartley shouted. "I must save the Lion Hunter before he is swept downstream!"

Hartley jumped into the river and pulled Daniel to safety on the bank.

As he lay there, Daniel
knew he had to think quickly,
or Hartley would realize
he wasn't strong after all.

"I told you once that I'm too powerful to need your help!" Daniel bellowed. "You have insulted me for the last time! That is your last mistake! I will call my servants to chase you from the jungle!"

"No!" shrieked Hartley. He was so terrified that he ran deep into the jungle, where Daniel couldn't follow.

"Finally," Daniel said. "I can be myself and do as I please again. No rules to follow made by someone who thinks they're stronger than me."

After a while, Hartley finally stopped running and collapsed against a tree, exhausted.
"I'm so tired," he panted, "but I can't let the Lion Hunter find me!"

Just then, a fox poked his head out of
a nearby tree trunk.
 "Hi," he said. "My name is *Wiley*.
What is the matter, King of the Beasts?
         May I be of some assistance?"

Hartley told Wiley the story of his experiences with the Lion Hunter.

"My dear King," said Wiley, "from your description, that animal was only a donkey. You're much more powerful than a donkey!"

"Really...?" said Hartley. "Just a donkey? Will you come with me to teach this donkey a lesson?"

"Yes," said Wiley. "Let's go see what this Lion Hunter...er...donkey is made of."

The two new friends found Daniel grazing by the riverbank.

Daniel saw them coming and realized that the fox had probably told Hartley that he was just a donkey.

Once again, he'd have to think fast.

"Thank you, Servant Fox, for bringing me back my lion!" shouted Daniel Hartley looked at Wiley, surprised.

"What? You tricked me!"

As he turned to run, Wiley reached out and grabbed him.

"Don't run, O Powerful King of the Beasts!" laughed Wiley. "This donkey is trying to trick you. Any beast of the jungle knows the fox is no one's servant.

This donkey is not my master. *Nor* is he yours!"

Hartley turned to Daniel.
"Why did you trick me?" he growled.
"I saved your life twice.
I was your friend!"

Daniel hung his head. "I'm sorry," he said.
"I was afraid because you are a mighty lion
and I'm just a donkey..."

"I'm very angry with you!" the lion roared.

Wiley stepped in.
"Be kind, King of Beasts," he said.
"This donkey is young.
Forgive him and send him on his way."

"You're right," said Hartley. "He is young and scared and far from home. I forgive you, Daniel. Try to remember to be as kind to others as I have been to you."

"Thank you, Hartley," Daniel said. "It's not nice to trick others, and I'll remember to be kind to everyone."
"Very good, my young friend," said Hartley. "Now you should go home to your family. They will be worried about you."

"I will," said Daniel. "I can't wait to get home!"

"I must be on my way too," said Wiley.
"Be careful, Daniel...
The next beast you meet may
not be as kind as Hartley."

With that, Wiley and Hartley left Daniel to ponder his behavior. He decided that even though he had been free from responsibilities, the family rules had been made to protect him from danger. He also knew that if he had to depend on tricks to get by, then surely he was not ready to be on his own.

Most important of
all, he knew that nothing was
as wonderful as the love and
support of his own family.

Questions

1. Why did Daniel want to be on his own?

2. Was Daniel a smart Donkey?

3. What did Daniel decide to do when Hartley's loud roar scared him? Did it work?

4. Was Wiley a good friend to Hartley? Was Wiley a good friend to Daniel?

5. Why did Daniel want to go home?

Application

1. Do you think you should always be able to do as you please?

2. Are you experienced enough to be on your own without the help and advice of your family and friends?

3. Would you forgive a person who has tricked you?

4. Why do you think families have rules to follow?

Live action version of this story
is also available on *video*.